Beck and the
Great Berry Battle

This edition published by Parragon in 2011

Parragon
Queen Street House
4 Queen Street
Bath, BA1 1HE, UK

ISBN 978-1-4454-2259-6

Printed in China.

Beck and the
Great Berry Battle

WRITTEN BY

Laura Driscoll

ILLUSTRATED BY

Judith Holmes Clarke

&

The Disney Storybook Artists

Bath · New York · Singapore · Hong Kong · Cologne · Delhi
Melbourne · Amsterdam · Johannesburg · Auckland · Shenzhen

Two tiny Never fairies
zipped through the forest.

"Oh, Beck," one of the fairies
said to the other, "thank you so
much for coming with me." She
looked terribly worried. "We just
don't know what to do. A baby
raccoon turned up in the gardens
this morning, and he started digging
up Rosetta's mint! We chased him

off, but he didn't go far. Now he's sitting on a tree stump by Havendish Stream and he won't budge. None of the other animal-talent fairies can understand a word he's saying!"

Beck smiled. "Don't worry, Latia," she said. "We'll figure it out."

Latia breathed a sigh of relief. "Well, if any fairy in Never Land can figure it out, it's you!"

All of the fairies agreed: Beck was one of the finest animal-talent fairies in Pixie Hollow. Like all the animal-talent fairies, Beck had a gift for talking to animals. Birdcalls, mouse squeaks, squirrel and chipmunk chatter – they were as clear and easy for Beck to understand as words and sentences.

Beck was especially good at talking to baby animals. Even when an animal was too young to speak, Beck could understand it.

When Beck and Latia came to Havendish Stream, a dozen animal-talent fairies were hovering around a tiny raccoon. He sat on a tree stump clutching a stalk of Rosetta's mint.

"Beck's here!" Latia called.

"Oh, thank goodness!" cried Fawn.

Beck flew up in front of the baby raccoon. "Hello, there," Beck said in Raccoon. "I'm Beck. What's your name?"

The little raccoon whimpered.

Then he buried his face in his paws. He rubbed his nose in the stalk of mint he had picked from Rosetta's garden.

"Oh, don't cry!" Beck said. She stroked the raccoon's furry head.

"Hey, now," said Beck, smiling. "Don't you want to play a game with me?"

Raising his head, the little raccoon looked at Beck for the first time. She smiled encouragingly. "That's right," she said. "I know the perfect game for us to play. It's called Find the Fairy!"

With that, Beck took off at top speed. She looped around behind the raccoon and tapped him on the shoulder. "Here I am!" she cried. The raccoon squeaked in surprise and turned around, but Beck was already gone.

The little raccoon peered up at the sky. Meanwhile, Beck quietly landed by the raccoon's paw. She reached up, tweaked his toe, and cried, "No, *here* I am!"

The little raccoon let out a chittering noise: raccoon laughter.

Beck grinned. She flew up to face him again. "That's a good game, isn't it?" she said. "Now let's start again. What's wrong?"

There was a pause, and the fairies

held their breath. Then the
raccoon replied.

"Lost!" He stared at Beck with
wide eyes.

"Oh, dear. Well, where do you
live?" Beck asked.

"Live...," the raccoon started. He
looked down at the mint stalk he
still held. "Live here!" he said. "Live...
in mint."

"Huh," said Beck. She looked at the fairies who were gathered around. Everyone looked as confused as she felt.

"What did he say?" asked Latia.

"He said that he lives in mint," Beck told her. "But that doesn't make any sense!"

"In mint?" replied Latia thoughtfully. "I wonder if he means... Oh, Beck! I know where he lives!"

"Remember when Rosetta planted her mint patch a few years ago?" Latia asked Beck. They were flying through the woods with the raccoon trailing after them. "Well, she asked me to find her some wild mint seeds from the forest. I got them from a mint patch near a tree on the edge of Pixie Hollow. I just bet his family lives in that tree!"

"That would explain why he was so interested in Rosetta's mint patch to begin with," Beck said. "It must have reminded him of –"

"Home!" cried the little raccoon. He took off running. Beck and Latia looked up and saw the big hollow tree. And playing in the mint leaves at the bottom was another baby raccoon. The two young raccoons tumbled in a heap at the foot of the tree, squeaking happily.

Beck explained everything to the baby raccoon's mother, who thanked her again and again. Then she waved goodbye to the baby raccoon, and she and Latia flew off in the direction of the Home Tree.

As they were flying over a thicket, Beck spotted Grandmother Mole coming out of an underground tunnel.

"Oh, Latia, why don't you go on without me?" Beck suggested. "I want to pay a visit."

Grandmother Mole was the

oldest female mole in Never Land, and a very dear friend.

"Hello, Grandmother," Beck said in Mole.

"Beck? Is that you?" asked Grandmother Mole.

"Yes, it's me," Beck replied. "I was just flying by. How's everything underground?"

"Oh, just fine," Grandmother Mole replied. "But there's exciting news! One of our own just had babies. Four beautiful and perfect baby moles. You should come by and teach them to play peekaboo."

Beck smiled. "That sounds wonder –"

Just then, old Grandfather Mole

climbed out of the tunnel opening and bumped right into Beck. "Oops!" he said. "Pardon me, sir! Wasn't watching where I was going, I guess!"

Then Grandfather Mole waddled off. Grandmother Mole giggled at his blunder. Beck couldn't help giggling, too.

After saying farewell to Grandmother Mole, Beck flew

to the Home Tree. She was filled with happiness.

Then, just as Beck flew over the river, she heard it. A cry. A cry for her? As she slowed, it got louder.

"Beck! Be-e-e-e-eck! Wait! Wait up!" the voice called.

Beck stopped and hovered in mid-air. She turned to look behind her and saw a young hummingbird headed straight for her at full speed. "Beck! Help! He-e-e-e-elp!"

The young hummingbird

tried to slow down, but he was going too fast. He smashed right into Beck.

"Twitter!" Beck exclaimed in Bird. "What in the world is going on?"

"I'm s-s-sorry about that, B-B-Beck!" Twitter chirped. He nervously darted to and fro in the air. Still dazed from the midair crash, Beck was getting dizzy trying to keep her

eye on Twitter. "It's j-j-just that you've g-g-got to help us. It's an e-e-emergency!"

Beck smiled. How many times had she heard that word – "emergency" – from Twitter before? Twitter was a sweet, good and earnest little bird. But sometimes he got overexcited for no reason. Beck suspected that this was one of those times.

"Okay, Twitter," she said. "What is it? I'm listening."

Twitter zigged this way and zagged that way in the air. "I'm telling you," he said, "it's an emergency! It's –" Twitter looked nervously over one wing, then the other. He flew right up to Beck's left ear and whispered, "It's the *chipmunks*."

"The chipmunks?" Beck said at a normal volume. "What about them?"

"Shhh!" Twitter cringed. "Not so loud! They might be listening. They're everywhere."

Twitter shot glances over both wings again. Then he continued. "They're so grabby and strange. I think they have it in for all us birds. They come right up into the trees and shrubs, and they gather all the seeds and acorns and berries in sight. And then they don't eat the stuff. They carry it away with them to their underground nests. I think they're hoarding all that food just so the birds can't have it. Why would they do that, Beck? Why?"

Beck couldn't help herself. She smiled. Then she giggled.

Twitter was confused. "What's so funny?" he asked Beck. "This is serious!"

Beck fought back another giggle. "I'm sorry, Twitter," she said kindly. "I know you're upset. But there's no reason to be. The chipmunks mean no harm. Some animals, like birds, eat food as they find it. But other animals, like chipmunks, store some of the food they find. They save it until they need it. Then they eat it."

Twitter looked at Beck in surprise. "They do?" he asked.

Beck nodded. "Mm-hmm. The chipmunks don't have it in for the birds. Besides, there's plenty of food to go around."

Twitter thought about what Beck had told him. "Okay. Thanks, Beck!" he exclaimed. Then he zipped out of

sight.

"You're welcome!" Beck called after him. She shook her head and smiled.

Just as quickly as he had come, Twitter was gone.

That afternoon, Beck was sitting alone in the tearoom, waiting for the other animal-talents to arrive.

She looked around the room. Her friend Tink was across the way with the pots-and-pans talents. She saw Rosetta fly in and join her friends at the garden-talent table. She watched Dulcie, a baking-talent fairy, serve star-shaped butter cookies all around.

Beck was seated next to one of the floor-to-ceiling windows. She was gazing outside when Fawn sat down next to her. There was a bright purple stain on one shoulder of her dress.

Beck giggled. "What happened to you?" she asked.

Fawn reached for the teapot in the centre of the table and poured herself a cup of peppermint tea. "A berry fell on me," she explained. "Just as I landed in the courtyard – *splat!*" Fawn shrugged. "Just bad luck, I guess."

Beck shrugged, too. Never fairies were used to dodging all sorts of things falling from above. Raindrops falling from the sky. Leaves or branches falling from trees. Berries falling from

shrubs. They had to be careful.

Terra, Madge and Finn were the next animal-talent fairies to come to the table. They helped themselves to tea. Dulcie flew over with a plate of cookies. Everyone reached for one at the same time.

Then Cora flopped into the last empty seat with a frustrated sigh. Bright purple juice soaked the top of her head. It dripped down her forehead and off the ends of her long, blonde hair. It was smeared on the sides of her face, where she had tried to wipe it away.

"You too, Cora?" Fawn asked. She pointed to the big purple splotch on her own dress.

"Berry?" Cora said.

Fawn nodded.

Beck wrinkled her brow. "What a strange coincidence," she said. "Two fairies hit by berries in the same day."

Finn stared over Beck's shoulder. "Make that three fairies," she said.

Beck turned to see a sparrow man with a big purple stain on his left leg at the art-talent table.

"I count four," said Madge. Across the room a decoration-talent fairy was wiping purple juice from the back of her neck.

"Uh... no," said Fawn. "Five." She nodded at the tearoom door, where Lympia, a laundry fairy, had two purple splotches – one on her right arm and one on her left wing.

What in the world was going on?

"This is no coincidence," said Beck. "Five fairies hit by berries in the same day? In the same *afternoon?*"

Just then, a loud *tap-tapping* sound made all six animal-talents jump in their seats. They turned towards the window. Outside, peeking in at them, was Twitter.

Madge reached over and swung open the window. Twitter landed on the sill.

"B-B-Beck!" he chirped, short of breath. "Come qu-qu-quick! It's an emergency!"

All the animal-talent fairies smiled

at Beck. They knew that Beck was the only fairy with the patience to calm the little bird.

"A battle has broken out!" Twitter chirped. "B-B-Beck, you've got to do something! You've g-g-got to stop it!"

Beck frowned. "A battle?" she

said doubtfully.

"Yes, a battle!" he exclaimed. "A berry battle!"

4

Beck hurried out of the tearoom. She zipped through the Home Tree lobby and out the front door. "Twitter," Beck called to the little bird, "what do you m—"

Out of the corner of her eye, she spied a berry falling toward her. She dodged to her right. The berry just missed her left shoulder and landed – *splat!* – on the ground.

"What do you mean, a berry battle?"
Beck asked.

"The chipmunks stole the nest!"
cried Twitter. He launched excitedly
into a long explanation. But he was
chirping so quickly, Beck could only

understand bits and pieces.

"Okay, okay, Twitter," Beck calmly interrupted him. "Let's do this: why don't you *show* me what you're talking about?"

Without another word, Twitter turned and flew away. Beck hurried after him.

Before long, Twitter stopped and perched on the branch of a blackberry bush. Beck landed next to him. She looked around. Nothing seemed out of the ordinary. The forest was perfectly quiet. Beck's curiosity bubbled over. "Twitter," she began.

But Twitter shushed her. He pointed a wing toward the clearing at the foot of the blackberry bush.

"Watch," he whispered.

So Beck watched and waited. In a few moments, a chipmunk scampered out from behind a hawthorn tree. He looked to his left, then his right. He looked up into the trees. Then he ran across the clearing toward the blackberry bush. In the centre of the clearing, the chipmunk paused.

Suddenly, the blackberry bush seemed to spring to life. It was full of hummingbirds!

Beck watched as the hummingbirds worked together to launch a storm of blackberries in the direction of the clearing. Some hooked to the left or right and others often went backwards. But most of them flew

directly at the chipmunk. He barely had time to turn away before they hit: one on his tail, one on his head and three more on his back.

Dripping berry juice, the chipmunk scampered out of the clearing. He disappeared behind the hawthorn tree.

"Hooray!" A round of cheerful hummingbird chirps rose from the blackberry bush.

Shocked by what she had seen, Beck leaped off the branch. For once, Twitter was right. This was an emergency!

"Stop! Stop!" she called as she flew out in front of the blackberry bush.

"What are you doing? Why would you do that to that chipmunk?"

"Oh, good day to you, Beck," came a voice from the blackberry bush. Suddenly, from a low branch, out flew Birdie, one of the oldest hummingbirds in Pixie Hollow. "I see you've heard about our... *problem*," Birdie said, hovering next to Beck.

Beck shrugged. "Well, I've heard that there *is* a problem," she said. "But I don't understand. What's going on?"

Birdie sighed. "We have to be able to defend ourselves. Don't we?"

"Defend yourselves from whom?" Beck asked.

"From the chipmunks, of course,"
Birdie replied. "They stole one of our
nests! One minute it was here – right
on one of these very branches. The
next minute it was gone! They can't
just steal one of our nests. And until
they give it back or say they're sorry,
they're not welcome in our shrubs.
And if they get too close... well... just
let them try!"

Beck decided to get the chipmunks' side of the story. When she found them, the chipmunks were plotting their revenge against the birds.

Beck tried to get them to calm down. She told them what the hummingbirds had said.

"Of course we didn't take their nest!" insisted Uncle Munk, one of the chipmunk elders.

"Great!" Beck replied. "Then it's

just a misunderstanding. It can all be settled peacefully."

But the chipmunks were mad. Already, too many of them had been berried.

"Everywhere we go in Pixie Hollow, we get hit with berries," Uncle Munk said. "We have to gather the food we need or we'll starve. We have to be able to defend ourselves. Don't we?"

With that, the chipmunks went back to their planning. Uncle Munk gave the instructions.

"Here's what we do," Uncle Munk said. "We fan out in all directions to circle the blackberry bush. Then we each start tunnelling underground

toward the bush. When we get to the roots, we pop up from underground. And we take the berries by force!"

Beck couldn't believe what she was hearing. She had to put an end to this before it got entirely out of hand.

Just then, a young chipmunk named Nan came running full speed around a tree trunk.

"Take cover!" screamed Nan as she ran.

Behind her, a shower of berries splattered on the forest floor, just missing her. Nan made a beeline for Uncle Munk's home. As more berries landed around them, the other chipmunks dove for cover. Beck was left alone, hovering over the entrance. She dodged one berry, then another.

A third berry sailed high over her head. Beck watched it as it carved a wide, high arc in the air, then began its fall back to earth. At the same moment, an old mole came strolling around a tree trunk, directly into the berry's path.

It was Grandfather Mole. The berry dropped right on his head. *Splat!*

Grandfather Mole stopped in his tracks. He reached up to feel his head. Finding it dripping wet, he turned and squinted in Beck's direction.

"Good day, sir," said the old mole. "Awfully large raindrops we're having today, aren't we?"

Within a few days, it

seemed to be raining berries all over
Pixie Hollow, all the time.

Some Never fairies started carrying
flower-petal umbrellas whenever
they went outside. But dainty
flower-petal umbrellas didn't hold up
against constant berry bombardment.

"Phooey!" said Silvermist, a water-
talent fairy, as she flew into the

Home Tree lobby. Her waterlily umbrella had been knocked inside out by the force of some direct hits. "This is the fourth umbrella I've gone through in two days!"

Beck led Silvermist to the umbrella-exchange table. "You can drop off your ruined umbrella," Beck explained. "And you can pick up a new umbrella. The garden fairies will use your old one for seeds. So everyone wins!"

The umbrella-exchange table had been Beck's idea. The Berry Battle was making big trouble for all the Never fairies. She and the other animal-talent fairies were working as hard as they could to end the war between the

hummingbirds and the chipmunks. But neither side was budging.

Rosetta helped Silvermist with her umbrella.

Then she noticed Beck glancing out the lobby window. "Beck, we've got this under control," she said kindly. "I mean, if there's somewhere else you need to be..."

"Thanks, Rosetta," Beck replied. She wanted to get outside to check in with the animals. Maybe something had changed. Maybe they had called a truce. She took a daisy-petal umbrella from the new-umbrella pile. "Mind if I borrow this?" she asked Rosetta.

Rosetta giggled. "Of course not,"

she replied.

Beck ventured outside. Almost right away, she heard a berry splatter on her open umbrella. She only had to go a short distance out in the open – just as far as the big oak tree with the split trunk. From there, she could continue her trip underground by using the tunnels that the animal-talent fairies had built.

Beck set out first for the chipmunk camp.

On her way, she met Fawn.

"Fawn!" Beck cried. Is there any news about the Berry Battle?"

Fawn frowned and shook her head. "Nothing good," she replied. "I just came from the hummingbird camp. They're still at it." Then Fawn's face brightened. "But now that I think of it, there is one piece of good news. You know the chipmunks' plan to tunnel their way to the blackberry bushes?" Fawn asked. "Well, that plan backfired."

"What do you mean 'backfired'?" Beck asked. "What happened?"

Just then, they heard a muffled scratching sound. Suddenly, a large paw punched through the tunnel floor. Then a furry head with a longish snout and beady eyes poked into the tunnel and looked around.

It was Grandmother Mole.

She spotted Beck and Fawn hovering in the tunnel.

"Oops!" said Grandmother Mole. She turned to talk to someone behind her. "Back up!" she said. "This isn't a chipmunk tunnel. It's the fairies' tunnel. Abort mission! Repeat: abort mission!"

Beck had no clue what kind of "mission" Grandmother Mole was leading. But she had a hunch it had something to do with the Berry Battle. And that could mean only one thing.

The moles had taken sides.

Beck's hunch turned out to be right. The moles had sided with the hummingbirds in the Berry Battle.

"But why?" Beck asked Grandmother Mole.

Grandmother Mole snorted. "Well," she said, "we didn't want to. But then those nasty chipmunks started digging all over the place. They bulldozed right through *our*

tunnels. They caused a lot of damage."
Grandmother Mole shrugged. "We
had to do *something*."

Beck was afraid to ask what
that "something" was. But she
asked anyway.

"When the chipmunks quit
digging for the day, we build lots
of side tunnels off their tunnels,"
Grandmother Mole explained. "They
come back the next day and they get
confused. They can't work out where
they left off." Grandmother Mole
stifled a giggle.

Beck didn't like the fact that there
were now more animals involved in
the Berry Battle. "So now it's the
hummingbirds and the moles against

the chipmunks," she said sadly.

At Beck's side, Fawn cleared her throat. "Actually, Beck," she said, "now it's the hummingbirds and the moles against the chipmunks and the *mice*."

Beck hurried on to the chipmunks' camp. She didn't want to believe that the mice had entered the war too.

But when Beck reached the chipmunks' camp, she found that it was true. Little Nan brought her up to date.

"The hummingbirds accidentally hit a baby mouse with a berry," Nan explained to Beck. "After that, the mice took our side."

Beck pulled Nan away from the worst of the fighting. They sat in the shelter of a hollow log. From there, they could see the animals battling it out.

It wasn't a pretty scene. The hummingbirds launched berries from the blackberry bush. Chipmunks fired back from the branches of a hawthorn tree. Mice scurried to-and-fro in the clearing between, collecting any

berries that fell to the ground still intact. Then, scurrying into the hawthorn tree, they passed those berries off to the chipmunks. The chipmunks used their tails to launch the berries back at the hummingbirds.

Beck pointed at a sparrow flying toward the chipmunks in the hawthorn tree. He was carrying a berry in his beak. "What's that sparrow doing?" she asked.

Nan followed Beck's gaze. "Oh," she replied. "I forgot to mention; the sparrows are on the hummingbirds' side. So are the chickadees and the cardinals."

Beck peered up into the air. Flocks of birds were dive-bombing the hawthorn tree. Berries were flying and falling everywhere. The Berry Battle was getting completely out of hand!

In the midst of it all, little Twitter flew right past Beck and Nan. He was so busy dodging falling berries that he didn't see them.

"Twitter!" Beck called out to him.

Twitter looked around.

"Over here!" Beck called. "Inside the log!"

Twitter flew over to the hollow log. "Whew!" he said, shaking some berry juice off his wing.

Then Twitter looked up and saw Nan.

"Oh!" said Twitter, staring at Nan. "It's a ch-ch-chipmunk!"

Beck smiled. She stepped out of the way so that Twitter and Nan could face each other.

"That's right, Twitter," said Beck in Bird. "It's a chipmunk. Her name is Nan." Beck turned and spoke in Chipmunk to Nan. "Nan, this is Twitter."

8

Beck watched Twitter and
Nan eye each other curiously. When
their eyes met, they both looked away.
Twitter stared at the ground. Nan
tugged at her ear. Then, slowly, their
gazes crept toward each other again.

Finally, Nan asked Beck, "Is he
your friend?"

"Yes, he is," replied Beck. "And
he loves to play hide-and-seek." Beck

knew that Nan also loved to play
hide-and-seek. And she knew that no
one had played any games at all since
the Berry Battle had begun.

"Really? Do you think he'd
play hide-and-seek with me?" Nan
asked shyly.

Beck turned to Twitter. "Nan
wants to know if you'll play
hide-and-seek with her," she said.

Twitter jumped a few inches off
the ground and hovered in mid-air.
"Yeah!" he replied. He was so excited,
he flew an upside-down loop. Beck
didn't have to translate that.
Nan understood.

She put her paws over her eyes.
Twitter flew down to the other

end of the log and hid behind a leaf. Nan opened her eyes and started looking. Just as she reached the leaf that Twitter was hiding behind, he popped up and flew off to the other side of the hollow log. Nan followed him.

Beck giggled as she watched them go. Twitter and Nan were so excited about making friends, they had forgotten all about her. She turned and looked out towards the berry battlefield. She sighed. If only the grown-up animals could put aside their differences as easily as the young ones, she thought.

In the distance, she spotted

Terence, a fairy-dust-talent sparrow man. He was struggling to fly through the shower of berries. In his arms he carried a dried minipumpkin canister full of fairy dust.

Terence gave out the daily doses

of fairy dust to the Never fairies. Each fairy got one level teacupful every day. It was an important job. Without fairy dust, fairies could only fly about a foot at a time. But with fairy dust, they could fly as long and as far as they wanted.

Beck guessed that Terence was on his way back to the Home Tree from the mill. He was trying to dodge berries as he flew. Beck took off to see if she could help him. But as she did, she saw a large berry fall right on Terence's canister and knock it out of his hands. The canister fell to the ground and fairy dust spilled everywhere.

"Oh, Terence," Beck said when she

reached his side. "Are you all right?"

Terence looked very unhappy. "I'm fine," he answered glumly. "But this fairy dust is wasted."

A thin layer of fairy dust had fallen on an anthill. Beck watched as all the ants that had been sprinkled with dust took to the air and flew around. Then she noticed a couple of spiders and an earthworm hovering in the air next to her.

Beck couldn't help laughing at the strange sight. "At least someone's getting some use out of it," she said.

Terence wasn't amused. "Yeah," he said. "But now – Oh, watch out!" He pulled Beck out of the path of

a falling blackberry. "Now I have to make another trip back to the mill." He sighed a heavy sigh. "This Berry Battle is out of control! What do you think would get them to stop fighting?" he asked.

At that very moment, Beck heard Nan and Twitter crying for help.

Beck wheeled around. A large hawk was perched atop the log that Twitter and Nan had been playing in. He bent over to poke his sharp beak into the hollow interior.

Twitter and Nan were cornered.

9

Beck sprang into action.

She flew straight for the hawk, across the berry battlefield. "Hold your fire!" she shouted as she flew down the front lines of the Berry Battle. "I repeat, hold your fire!"

Beck knew she couldn't fight off the hawk herself. She would need help. But none of the chipmunks or hummingbirds had seen that Nan and Twitter were in trouble. Beck waved her arms wildly. She had to get the animals' attention!

She pointed at the hawk. "Stop fighting and look!" she shouted.

Slowly but surely, the warring animals noticed Beck. They all looked where she was pointing. They saw the hawk. And then they saw Nan and Twitter.

All at once, the Berry Battle came to a halt.

Beck reached the hollow log first. The hawk had smashed in one end, blocking the exit. That left only the one open end, which he was guarding. He was hunched over, with his head upside down, peering

into the log. He was too big to go in
after the young animals. Instead, he
waited for them to try to escape.

Beck swooped past the hawk's
face, flying dangerously close to his
curved beak. She got his attention.
The hawk sat upright as his eyes

followed her. She just hoped to distract him long enough for the youngsters to get away.

The hummingbirds saw what Beck was trying to do. Within moments, dozens of hummingbirds swarmed around the hawk. They poked at the top of his head with their long, pointy beaks. They flew in front of his face, zigging and zagging.

Other birds moved in to help. Sparrows, chickadees and cardinals circled over the hawk's head. Then, one by one, they dive-bombed the hawk with berries. Several berries hit the hawk on the head. One hit him right between the eyes.

But the berries didn't bother the

hawk. He barely noticed them. They were tiny to a bird of his size. In fact, even as the birds dropped berries on him, the hawk continued peering into the log.

The animals had to find another way to distract him.

The chipmunks launched the next attack. They scurried onto tree branches hanging directly over the log. Then two chipmunks dove onto the back of the hawk's head. He stood bolt upright on the log. The hawk raised his right wing and brushed at his head, trying to get the chipmunks off. But the chipmunks held on.

Meanwhile, behind the hawk's back, Uncle Munk sneaked up to the log. He crept closer and closer to the open end. While the hawk was distracted, he scurried up to the opening.

"Psst!" he whispered to Nan and Twitter. "Come on! Follow me!"

Even though he couldn't understand Uncle Munk's words, Twitter zipped forwards.

But Nan didn't follow.

"Nan!" Uncle Munk whispered. "Come on! Now's our chance!"

Nan was frozen with fear. She huddled against the back of the log, trembling, her eyes wide.

"You go ahead!" Uncle Munk

whispered to Twitter, waving him on. Twitter hesitated. He didn't want to leave his new friend behind. But Twitter felt he should do what Uncle Munk wanted.

So Twitter flitted past Uncle Munk and out of the log. The hawk, still trying to shake the chipmunks off his head, didn't even see him fly past. Twitter landed on a blackberry branch. The hummingbirds flocked to him to make sure he was okay.

"I'm f-f-fine," he told everyone. "But Nan...."

Nan was still trapped inside the log. Uncle Munk stood at the opening, trying to convince her to come out.

"You can do it, Nan," Beck heard Uncle Munk say. "Just put one paw in front of the other. Come towards me."

He was so focused on Nan, he didn't notice that the hawk had shaken the chipmunks off. They ran for cover as the giant bird turned back to the log. He spotted Uncle Munk.

Beck and all the animals gasped.

"Uncle Munk!" Beck called. "Run!"

Uncle Munk looked up. The hawk's eyes were glued to him. Then, in one sudden, lightning-fast movement, the hawk lunged at Uncle Munk. The chipmunk dodged the bird's hooked beak and scurried away.

The hawk leaned over to look

inside the log once more. Seeing Nan still there, he settled down to wait her out.

The animals had to try something else. Birdie the hummingbird had an idea. As Beck had done, she swooped past the hawk's face to get his attention. Then she landed on the ground a few feet in front of the log. She hopped along, dragging one wing behind her. The hawk watched her, cocking his head. He leaned forwards to get a closer look.

"She's pretending she's hurt!" Beck said to Uncle Munk. "She's figuring that hawks go for the easiest prey first. Young animals are easy targets. But injured animals are even easier. She's trying to lure the hawk off the log – to get him to go for her."

What Birdie was doing was terribly dangerous. She was risking her own life to save Nan's.

Beck and Uncle Munk watched as Birdie turned her back on the hawk. Very slowly, she hopped away from the log. The hawk leaned over again to look in at Nan. Then he looked up at Birdie. He looked back and forth between his two choices of prey.

The hawk spread his wings and leaped off the log. He soared the short distance to Birdie and got ready to drop onto the little bird. But at the last possible moment, Birdie took to the air. She flew a few feet, landed again and continued hopping along, dragging her wing. The hawk flew after her and pounced again. Again, Birdie took off at the last second. "Now is our chance," whispered Uncle Munk. With the hawk out of the way, he dashed over to the log.

"Nan, come with me! You can do it!" he told her.

With a little more encouragement, Uncle Munk got Nan out of the log. They ran away as fast as they could.

Within seconds, they were safe,
hidden behind the trunk of an
oak tree.

"Birdie!" Beck called out. "Birdie,
they're clear!"

Birdie heard Beck's call and knew
that Nan was safe. So when the hawk
pounced again, she took to the air.
This time, she sped away.

The confused hawk watched her fly
out of his reach. He looked around
for other prey. But of all the animals
and Beck were safely out of sight.

Finally, the hawk gave up and
flew away.

All around the clearing, the

animals breathed sighs of relief. They had outwitted the hawk. They had saved Nan and Twitter.

And they had done it by working together.

10

The animals stayed hidden for a few minutes to make sure the coast was really clear. Then, one by one, they all came out of their hiding places.

They gathered in the clearing, making a wide circle around Nan and Twitter, Uncle Munk, Birdie and Beck.

"Are you two all right?" Beck

asked the youngsters. They looked unharmed. But Beck could sense that they were still getting over their fear – especially Nan.

"I'm okay," Twitter replied. "Are *you* okay, Nan?" Twitter asked his new friend. Beck translated for him.

Nan nodded but didn't speak.

"She'll be fine," Uncle Munk said cheerfully. He looked up at Birdie. "And it's thanks to you, old bird. You risked everything for Nan. How can we thank you?"

Beck told Birdie what Uncle Munk had said. Birdie brushed off the praise with a wave of her wing. "Nonsense," she replied. "You're the one who got Twitter safely out of that log. You are due as much credit as I am." She turned to Beck. "And you! What if you hadn't been here, Beck? We were all so wrapped up in our" – Birdie paused – "*argument*. We might not have seen that the little ones were in trouble... until it was too late."

Beck smiled a big smile. Her glow flared with a mixture of embarrassment and pride. "Oh, don't mention it," she said. But secretly, Beck was very glad to think she might have been of some help. Especially after days and days of trying to end the Berry Battle – with no luck.

"I'm just glad this whole thing is over," Beck said with a chuckle.

She looked at Uncle Munk, then at Birdie. "It is over, isn't it?" she asked them. "The Berry Battle, I mean."

Birdie shifted her weight from one foot to the other. "Well," she said, "there is the small matter of the nest." She looked over at Uncle Munk. "The missing nest, that is. I *do* think it would be nice if they would return it."

Uncle Munk stared at Beck with wide eyes while she translated. "But we didn't even take that nest!" he cried. "Honestly! I don't know why they think we did."

The whole clearing was silent.

All the other animals waited to

hear what would happen next.

Then, on the outer ring of the circle of animals, there was a slight commotion.

"Oh, pardon me," came a friendly voice. "Oh, excuse me. Oh! Bit of a gathering here, eh?"

The front row of animals parted. Out from behind them strolled old Grandfather Mole. Moseying past Beck, he tipped his hat. "Good day, sir!" he said to her. "Somewhat crowded in the forest today, isn't it?"

It took a few moments for Beck to notice that his hat was not a hat at all. It was an upside-down, hollowed-out mass of moss, plant bits and spiderwebs.

It was a hummingbird nest!

"Um, Grandfather Mole?" she called. "Where did you get that...

thing on your head?"

All around Beck, the animals realized what it was. They gasped and pointed at Grandfather Mole's head.

Birdie's beak hung open.

"What?" Grandfather Mole said. "Do you mean my hat?" He reached up and took it off. He held it out at arm's length. "Isn't it a fine hat? I found it a few days ago. I was out for a walk. I strolled by that blackberry bush over yonder." Grandfather Mole pointed to the hummingbirds' bush – the very bush that the missing nest had been in.

"This hat was on the ground underneath it. Oh, naturally, I looked around to see if anyone might have dropped it. But there was no one in sight. So I picked it up and tried it on. It fit perfectly!" He put the nest back on his head. "I'm wearing it out for the first time this afternoon. With all this strange weather we've been having, it's come in very handy."

Beck could not believe her ears. She looked over at Birdie and Uncle Munk. They seemed equally amazed. Had the forest really been divided over a silly misunderstanding?

"Well, good day to you," said Grandfather Mole as he continued on his walk. The animals watched him walk away with a hummingbird nest on his head.

Then, suddenly, Beck and all the animals began to laugh.

Their laughter was so loud that

several Never fairies in the Home
Tree, a fair distance away, heard
the sound.

It was the sound of the end of the
Berry Battle.